SKOLO
THE BLADED
MONSTER

With special thanks to Michael Ford
To Michael Nolan

www.beastquest.co.uk

ORCHARD BOOKS
338 Euston Road, London NW1 3BH
Orchard Books Australia
Level 17/207 Kent St, Sydney, NSW 2000

A Paperback Original
First published in Great Britain in 2014

Beast Quest is a registered trademark of Beast Quest Limited
Series created by Beast Quest Limited, London

Text © Beast Quest Limited 2014
Cover and inside illustrations by Steve Sims © Beast Quest Limited
2014

A CIP catalogue record for this book is available from
the British Library.

ISBN 978 1 40832 930 6

3 5 7 9 10 8 6 4 2

Printed and bound by CPI Group (UK) Ltd, Croydon, CR0 4YY

The paper and board used in this paperback are natural recyclable
products made from wood grown in sustainable forests. The
manufacturing processes conform to the environmental regulations of
the country of origin.

Orchard Books is a division of Hachette Children's Books,
an Hachette UK company

www.hachette.co.uk

SKOLO
THE BLADED
MONSTER

BY ADAM BLADE

ORCHARD

TH

THE FOREST
OF FEAR

WESTERN OCEAN

THE

THE RUBY DESERT

SP

STORY ONE

Avantia is finally at peace.

Thanks to Tom, no Beasts attack our borders and our enemies are kept at bay. With no dangers to assail us, I intend to travel the kingdom, touring the beautiful landscape and greeting my subjects.

But my old friend, Aduro, looks serious. Of course, since his magic was taken away, he's been a different man. At least, I hope that is the only cause for his worry. Even without his powers, he is still wise. I think he senses things that others do not. And on the road, danger is never far off...

So away we go, first to the south and to Spindrel. It has been many years since I visited that city. May good fortune favour us, and Evil remain a distant memory.

King Hugo

CHAPTER ONE

LET THE TOURNAMENT COMMENCE

Tom stood in a field outside the walls of Spindrel, among the tents of the royal camp. He watched the flags flutter in the breeze and courtiers mill about. The air was alive with chatter about the upcoming jousting tournament, organised in the king's honour. Tom was as excited as anyone – the ride from Avantia's capital had taken several days, and the tournament was just what the royal party needed.

He was tightening the saddle of his stallion, Storm, by the water trough, letting his eyes travel past the huge walls of the city. *Spindrel has completely changed since the last time I was here*, he thought. Back then, its drab grey walls had almost blended in with the slabs of mountain rock behind them. But those were the days when the spider Beast, Arachnid, had been plaguing the city and the people were cowering in their homes.

Tom grinned. This time the town was showing its visitors a warm welcome, with bunting hanging from the windows and feasts laid out on trestle tables in the streets.

He left his stallion drinking at the trough and went to find Elenna. As he crossed the tournament ground, he saw King Hugo standing by the makeshift seating platform the townsfolk had erected. He was laughing with Aduro, his former wizard. It was good to see the king looking relaxed after so many recent

threats to Avantia. This tour of the kingdom had been Aduro's idea, and Tom thought it an excellent one – there was no better way to make the people feel safe and protected than for their king to visit them in person.

Elenna was crouching beside her wolf, Silver, near the end of the jousting yard, brushing brambles and dirt from his grey coat. Behind her almost all the seating was filled already – young and old, rich and poor had received the heralds' summons and travelled from neighbouring villages to watch the tournament laid on for King Hugo.

"Looks like a full house," Tom said.

Elenna grinned. "Everyone loves jousting. Don't you wish you were taking part?"

"It wouldn't be fair," Tom said with

a sigh. "I have the Golden Armour, remember?"

Though his suit of armour was actually back at King Hugo's castle, its powers never left Tom – he doubted any warrior stood a chance against his magical abilities.

"I suppose you're right," said Elenna, and nodded at something beyond Tom. "Captain Harkman will put forward the king's champion today."

Tom turned sideways and saw the captain of the King's Guard talking to his top knight, Oliver, who wore full silver armour. As he tested out different lances, his eye caught Tom's through his open visor. Oliver raised a lance in greeting and Captain Harkman waved.

"Good luck!" Tom called to Oliver.

"He'll need it," muttered a low

voice from the stands. Tom saw it was a man drinking from a flagon. "Spindrel boasts the finest jousters in the kingdom!"

"Care to wager on that?" shouted another voice – one of Hugo's courtiers.

"Indeed I will!" replied the first man.

Tom laughed at their good-natured banter. A high-pitched whinny caught his attention and he recognised it at once. Glancing over to Storm, Tom saw another knight, a huge man in full armour, at the horse's side, clutching his reins and stroking his nose with a gauntleted hand. Strangely, the armoured man's helmet was completely closed, even though soldiers didn't normally shut their visors until just before the joust.

Storm bucked a little, as if uneasy.

"It's all right, boy!" said Tom, rushing over before the man got a nasty kick. "He's only a jouster."

The knight had moved away by the time Tom reached the stallion's side. Tom watched him go with a shudder.

No wonder Storm is jittery, he thought. *That man was enormous!*

The horse's nostrils flared as Tom patted his neck. "Nothing to worry about," Tom soothed.

Elenna had followed him. "Who was that?" she said. "Storm didn't seem to like him very much."

Tom shrugged. "Another competitor, I suppose. The tournament is open to all."

Elenna took her bow off her shoulder and tested the tension of its string. Beside her, Silver growled. "Not you as well!" she said. "I'm just getting ready for the archery contest."

Tom looked around for the knight again, but then a horn blew a long note and the crowd cheered.

"Let the tournament begin!" shouted King Hugo.

First came the duels. The finest of King Hugo's knights squared off against one another in exhibition fights, their weapons gleaming in the sunlight and clanging against each other until one knight yielded or fell.

Next was the archery contest. Targets were lined up at twenty paces for beginners, and fifty paces for the advanced competitors. Straight away it was clear there were two frontrunners – Elenna was one, of course. She scored bullseye after bullseye in the furthest target. But there was a blond boy too, perhaps a year or two older than Tom, who showed amazing skills. He too hit the centre of the targets, sometimes loosing a second arrow before the first had even found its mark. Sometimes his hands were a blur as he drew the

next shaft from his quiver while the
bowstring was still vibrating from
the previous shot. Each time he hit
the bullseye he would turn to the
cheering crowd with a bow.

"He's quite something, isn't he?"
said Dorina, an old woman at Tom's
side. She'd helped Tom and Elenna
on a previous Quest, and he had
chosen to watch the contest with her,

rather than at the king's bench as was his right as Master of the Beasts.

"He's a show-off!" said Tom.

Elenna obviously thought so too. Tom could see her glowering at the boy.

"I don't remember him from last time we visited," Tom went on.

"He's not from Spindrel," said Dorina. "All I know is his name – Shawn."

"A final test to decide the winner!" said Shawn, playing up to the crowd. He walked across to a boy with a fruit cart, and whispered something in his ear. The boy nodded, took a handful of apples from his cart and sprinted off, past both targets. He laid the apples in a row on a tree stump, then backed well away.

"Do you think you can hit one?"

Shawn asked Elenna.

For a moment, she looked unsure, squinting at the fruit. But she nodded. "You go first," she said.

Shawn grinned, drew an arrow, placed it against his bowstring and drew it back. After a deep breath, he fired. His arrow darted through the air, skimming the middle apple and toppling it from its perch.

"Incredible shot, if I say so myself," said Shawn, stepping back. "Your turn, girl."

Elenna looked like she was about to snap at him, but instead she stepped briskly forward, plucking two arrows from her quiver. In less than a heartbeat she let them fly.

Thud-thud!

Tom heard the sounds in quick succession and the crowd was silent.

"Well?" whispered Dorina in his ear. "Did she do it?"

The fruit-seller rushed back to the tree stump and bent to the ground. When he rose he was holding two arrows, each one threaded right through the centre of an apple. Elenna had hit two targets at once! The crowd roared and Elenna gave a small satisfied smile.

"Of course she did!" said Tom to Dorina.

Shawn's mouth was gaping, his face turning crimson.

"Not bad for a girl, huh?" said Elenna, looping her bow back over her shoulder.

Tom couldn't help the laugh that escaped his lips, earning a glare of pure hatred from Shawn.

"Elenna wins the archery contest!"

said King Hugo. "Now, it's time for the joust! Daltec – the prize, please!"

The young Wizard held out his arms, his lips moving in a spell. With a flash of light, a sword appeared, lying horizontal in his hands. Its silver blade shone in the sunlight, and its hilt was a heavy cross of gold studded with twinkling emeralds. The spectators could only gaze in wonder at such a magnificent and obviously valuable weapon.

"May the best jouster win!" said King Hugo.

The jousting tournament pitted the best of Captain Harkman's knights against the finest from around the kingdom. Each rode at the other down the lists, trying to knock their opponents from their saddles. Lances shattered, riders were unhorsed, and armour was dented as the knights did battle. Tom watched keenly, and from the start one knight stood out above the others – the strange black-clad figure who'd been petting Storm earlier. He rode down the lists on his flaxen-maned steed at a furious gallop, his lance-tip steady. He sent opponent after opponent tumbling to the ground without mercy. Soon there were only two riders left undefeated – this stranger who never lifted his visor, and Captain Harkman's star knight, Oliver. Then even Oliver went the same way as the rest, blasted from his horse's back by the stranger's unyielding lance.

Tom looked at Captain Harkman. "Better luck next time," he said.

"I might have to come out of

retirement myself!" muttered the captain.

"We have a victor!" said King Hugo. "Come, champion, and claim your prize!"

The black-armoured knight dismounted from his horse and strode towards the king's bench. His gait gave Tom an uneasy feeling – there was something weirdly familiar about the confident pacing steps, and from the way he moved, panther-like, Tom sensed a muscular figure lurking beneath the plates of steel.

The jouster knelt at the king's feet, and spoke some muffled words.

"I cannot accept your prize," he said.

A murmur passed through the crowd.

"Why not?" asked the king. "You

have bested our finest warriors."

"Not quite," the knight replied.
"There is one whom I have yet to
face."

He stood and turned, and pointed a
black finger straight at Tom.

CHAPTER TWO

THE JOUST

"Looks like you *will* be fighting today after all," said Elenna beside him.

"Me?" said Tom. "But..."

He saw King Hugo give a nod to Daltec, who clicked his fingers. A moment later, the Golden Armour appeared over Tom's body. He felt the helmet's weight on his head and he flexed his fingers in the golden gauntlets. Under the breastplate, he

felt his chest swell with pride. "Very
well," he said.

The black knight was already
marching back to his horse, so Tom
walked to Storm.

"Ready for a little play?" Tom said.
Storm shook his mane and neighed
as Tom climbed into the saddle. The

stallion twitched beneath him.

What's got into him today?

"Just trust me," said Tom. "I know we haven't done a lot of jousting before, but we've faced Beasts a lot more deadly."

He rode up to King Hugo and brought Storm to a halt beside the black knight.

"It will be an honour to challenge you," Tom said with a bow, "and to represent my king. Who is it I am facing, may I ask?"

The stranger grunted, and yanked his horse's head around, cantering to the far end of the lists.

Not very polite, is he? thought Tom grimly. *Well, let's teach him some manners.*

Tom took his place at the opposite end, and Elenna handed him a lance.

Storm still felt jittery beneath him.

"Be careful," said his friend. "I don't like the looks of this knight."

"Don't worry about me," said Tom. But as he gazed down the jousting yard at his opponent, he felt a shiver of dread. His father, Taladon, had died in a joust with a deadly knight. Perhaps it was no surprise that the memory returned to him now.

The horn blew and Tom dug his heels into Storm's sides.

Come on! he urged himself, heart thumping as the stallion lurched forward and his hooves pounded into a gallop.

The black knight did the same, leaning low over his horse's neck and levelling his lance. Tom struggled to stay balanced as they approached in the centre, and tugged the reins

harder than he intended, veering off
target at the last moment. He felt a
jolt of panic as his opponent's lance
passed his neck and his own hit
nothing but air. They thundered past
one another and the crowd let out
a collective gasp. At the far end, he
brought Storm around.

Just a practice run, he told himself,

though he knew he'd been lucky not to be hit. He pushed the fear aside.

They rode at each other once more, and straight away Tom felt clumsy again, as if the point of his lance were dragging him off-balance.

Something's not right, he thought to himself. It was as if he were a novice rider again, just learning the basics. He couldn't get steady in his saddle for a strike. He pulled back in the centre to avoid the black knight's lance and they passed one another again without a contact. Some of the spectators began to boo.

"Are you all right, Tom?" asked Elenna, who was waiting for him back at the start point.

Tom lifted his visor. "I'm not sure," he said, looking down the lists at his challenger. He still hadn't shown his face. *It must be hot in that helmet – hard to breathe. Why isn't he lifting the visor?*

"Maybe you shouldn't ride again," said Elenna.

Tom looked at his friend in alarm. To give up now would be the ultimate dishonour. He slammed down his visor, and gripped the lance firmly, pointing it right at the knight's heart. *I won't miss this time.*

He kicked Storm into a gallop, and almost toppled from the saddle as the stallion launched forward. He was slipping again, to the right, but now he realised why.

Oh no! The saddle's loose!

He barely managed to stay upright as Storm charged. His teeth rattled in his head and his lance-tip bobbed about all over the place. If he could just straighten up...

Crunch!

The blow slammed into Tom's chest, knocking his breath from his lungs and lifting him off the saddle. Tom felt his limbs flailing.

Slam!

He landed on his back, hard, and white light exploded behind his eyes.

For a moment, all he could do was

lie still, pain throbbing through his neck and back.

"Is he all right?" someone yelled.

Elenna, Tom realised.

"Give him air!" said Aduro's voice.

Tom heard hurried footsteps approaching, and managed to lift his visor. He sucked fresh air into his lungs and sat up slowly. The black knight was striding towards him, face still hidden, but reaching out a hand. In the background, he saw Captain Harkman trying to calm Storm while holding his reins.

"Lie still," said Elenna, rushing to his side before the black knight could help him up. "You might have broken something."

"I'm all right," said Tom, climbing to his feet. "Only wounded pride."

The black knight had stopped in his

tracks, and seemed to be staring at both of them through the narrow slit of his helmet. Then he turned away and marched back to King Hugo.

The king extended a hand. "Congratulations, champion," he said. "Now you have truly proved your worth."

The knight paused for a moment, then gripped the king's hand in his. Tom thought he saw King Hugo wince a little at the power of the stranger's grip.

"Daltec – the prize," said Hugo. "Stranger knight, you must dine with us tonight."

The knight shook his head slowly, stepped back from the bench, and walked over to his horse. The crowd watched with confused mumbling as he mounted, then began to ride away towards a forest in the distance at speed.

"Where's he going?" said Daltec. "He hasn't even got the sword!"

Soon the rider was a distant dot, and the spectators were starting to disperse from the stands.

"Why didn't he even show his face?" said Tom.

"You're just saying that because you lost," said Elenna with a sly grin.

Tom tried to grin back, but he couldn't muster a smile. Something wasn't right about that knight.

"I don't like this," he muttered. "Not one bit."

CHAPTER THREE
THE CHASE

As Tom was taking off his armour in his tent, the troubling questions mounted. Why would the knight go to all that effort to win, only to walk away? It didn't make sense. And that strange gait – where did he know it from?

As Tom was laying aside the golden gauntlets, Captain Harkman arrived at the open door holding Storm's

reins. "Next time, make sure your
saddle is on firmly before you sit on
it," he said sternly. "Even new recruits
know that, so I expect better from the
Master of the Beasts!"

The captain left, and Tom undid
the straps on his dented golden
breastplate. He eased it off with a

grimace and pulled up his tunic. A
purple bruise the size of a fist had
already formed over his breastbone
from where the black knight's lance
had thumped into him. He touched
it gingerly and a hiss of pain escaped
his teeth. Captain Harkman was right
– he should never have made such
a mistake. He could have ended up
with much worse than a nasty bruise.
What if he'd fallen beneath Storm's
hooves, or the lance had caught his
neck? He might not have lived to tell
the tale.

Tom took off the leg armour last,
frowning. *Hold on!* he thought. He did
remember tightening Storm's saddle
not long before the tournament
began. That meant that someone had
loosened it. *Of course!* Now he recalled
Storm's strange agitation around the

knight, before the contest had even begun. What if the black figure hadn't just been petting Storm? What if he'd been...

Don't be a sore loser, he told himself. *The contest is over and the knight has gone, anyway.*

Elenna's face appeared at the doorway. Silver was at her side.

"The court is gathering for dinner and the prize-giving ceremony. Are you ready?"

"Coming!" said Tom, jumping up and regretting it. His whole body ached from the tumble off Storm's back.

Outside, Tom almost bumped right into Daltec. The young wizard was frowning.

"Is there something the matter?" Tom asked him.

"Can you handle the prize-giving?" said Daltec. "It's just that the king... well...he seems to be rather poorly."

The hairs on Tom's neck prickled. It wasn't like King Hugo to be unwell.

"Take me to him," he said.

Daltec led the way through the camp to the king's tent. Two soldiers guarded the entrance but they parted their spears when Tom and Daltec approached.

Inside, the first thing Tom noticed was the rotten stench. The interior was dimly lit with sputtering candles, and King Hugo lay on a bed in just his under-tunic. He looked terrible, slick with sweat that matted his hair to his forehead. His eyes were wide enough to see the whites the whole way around his irises, and he groaned as he writhed weakly. Aduro

knelt beside him, a damp cloth in his
hand. Beside him were several books,
all open at various pages showing
different remedies.

Rather poorly? thought Tom in shock.
He looks close to death's door!

"What happened?" he said. "He was
fine not long ago at the joust."

Aduro shook his head. "We don't

46

know. He came to change and wash for dinner. Next thing, one of the guards heard him collapse and knock over his water bowl."

"Has anyone else been in here?" Tom asked.

Aduro shook his head again. "And he hasn't eaten anything bad, either." He gestured to the books with a wrinkled hand. "I've been looking for some cure, but this is unlike any disease or illness I've come across."

Tom felt a flash of horror as his mind recalled the previous few hours. He remembered the odd expression of pain on the king's face as he shook hands with the black knight. "So the last person to touch His Majesty before he became ill was the mystery jouster?" he said.

Aduro and Daltec shared a glance.

"I suppose so," said the young wizard, "but you don't think he had anything to do with this, do you?"

Tom told them about the issue with his saddle, and Aduro's face became graver by the second.

"We need to find the stranger knight," said Daltec. "At once! Send out word."

Aduro mopped King Hugo's gleaming brow with the cloth again. "I think that would be a bad idea," he said. "If the knight knows we're on to him, he'll make his escape even more quickly. Plus, we don't want word getting out about the king's condition. It could cause panic."

Tom realised the old counsellor was right. "Then I'll go with Elenna in secret," he said.

He was at the tent door when

Aduro called after him. "Don't delay, Tom. I'm not sure how long he's got."

Tom rushed to the banqueting tent, where he found Elenna seated at a bench surrounded by the young folk of Spindrel. All were listening intently – including Shawn, Tom noticed, even though the blond boy was trying to look uninterested.

"...but it wasn't Avantia we returned to," she was saying. "This was a kingdom ruled by Evil and called Tavania..."

Tom slid alongside her and whispered in her ear. "Story time's over," he said.

"A Beast?" Elenna whispered back.

Tom shook his head. "I'll explain on the way. Let's go."

In no time, they were on horseback, galloping through the meadows away from the camp. Storm, thankfully, was suffering no ill effects from the joust, and Silver raced beside them in a grey blur. The black knight's path was easy enough to follow where the grass was long, and Silver's nose did the rest in the barer patches. But then they came to an apple orchard some distance from the camp. There, the horse's hoofprints went one way, and the heavy footprints went the other.

"He dismounted here," said Tom, "and continued on foot."

"What sort of knight abandons his horse?" Elenna asked.

They followed the footprints as night fell over the landscape. Ahead loomed the treeline of a forest. Something lay on the ground

beside one of the trunks – a figure!
– and Tom steered Storm towards
it, drawing his sword. Perhaps the
knight had decided to take a rest,
thinking he'd made good his escape.

Well, I'll show him…

But as he closed in, Tom's hope
gave way to disappointment. It was
just the knight's suit of armour,
discarded on the ground.

"He must have decided to travel
light," said Tom. "And what sort
of knight discards both horse *and*
armour?" He answered his own
question: "Not a knight at all, I'll
wager."

"He hasn't left all the armour," said
Elenna. "Look, Tom – it's missing the
right gauntlet."

She was right. Tom sheathed his
sword, and used the power of the

51

golden helmet to stare into the forest.
Two hundred paces away, a shadow
flitted between the trees.

"I see him!" Tom cried. "Come on!"

Storm wouldn't be any use among
the low branches, so Tom slid off the
stallion's back. He sprinted through
the trees with Elenna and Silver at his
heels.

You won't get away! he thought, as he
leapt over a fallen trunk and ducked
a low branch. He could see the trees
give way to a clearing ahead, and
something huge looming through the
branches. The figure was standing in
the centre of the clearing, his back to
Tom, reaching for the sky.

As the figure turned, a shaft of dim
light caught his face – glowering and
marked with several deep scars. His
left eye drooped slightly with an area

of pink, burnt flesh. Tom skidded to
a halt and ducked behind a tree. He
heard Elenna gasp.

It was a face they'd hoped never to
see again.

Sanpao, the Pirate King!

CHAPTER FOUR

SANPAO'S PLOT

Sanpao hadn't spotted them. Tom pressed himself close to the tree and froze.

"What's he doing here?" whispered Elenna.

"Something evil," said Tom. "I knew I recognised that walk!"

He reached to draw his sword again, but Elenna grabbed his arm.

"Wait! You can't just rush out there!"

"Why not?" said Tom. "I'll make him pay!"

Elenna kept a firm grip on his arm. "Don't let anger cloud your judgement, Tom," she said. "We need him to tell us what he's done to King Hugo, so that we can work out how to undo it."

Tom let his breathing slow and his fury subside. Elenna was right, as always. He peered out from behind the tree again, and used his magic vision to focus on the gauntlet on Sanpao's right hand.

"There are tiny spikes on the palm of his gauntlet," he said to Elenna. "That must be how he struck down the king – with a poisoned handshake!"

"Cunning," said Elenna. "But how did he know he would even get close to King Hugo?"

Tom thought back to the joust, recalling the moment Sanpao had reached out to help him up. "He didn't," he said. "He meant to poison me."

Elenna was looking confused.

"Think about it," said Tom. "It was all a plot to kill me. Sanpao wanted to face me, remember? He'd already loosened my saddle so I'd fall. Then he reached to help me up with his right hand. But you got there first when I was on the ground."

"So the king was a last-minute change of plan," said Elenna.

Tom nodded. "Let's arrest him. Cover me."

Elenna quickly put an arrow to her bow as Tom crept out from their hiding place. He darted from tree to tree, getting closer all the time. As

his eyes drilled through the dusky
darkness, he realised that the huge
shape was Sanpao's flying pirate ship,
floating not far off the forest floor
and descending slowly. A gangplank
lowered from the deck.

*If I don't get there soon, Sanpao will
escape for good*, Tom thought.

He quickly came up with a plan.
First, he needed a distraction. He set
one foot on a broken branch, and let
his weight crack it in two. The sound
made Sanpao's head turn, his long,
spiked ponytail whipping round.
Tom sprinted away, magically fast,
harnessing the power of his golden
leg armour. He circled the clearing's
edge, then charged in from the
opposite direction. He saw pirates
swarming close to the deck-rails
above as the ship touched down, but

he headed straight for Sanpao, keeping his shoulder low.

Thump!

He barged into the Pirate King with all his speed and weight, and Sanpao collided with the ship's hull. The pirate fell to his knees, but was grinning when he looked back up at Tom.

"Hello, loser," he said. "Come for a rematch?"

Tom drew his sword and pointed it at Sanpao. "What poison did you use?" he asked.

Sanpao stood slowly, his grin widening. "You're too late," he said. "Nothing can be done for your king now – not even by Avantia's greatest so-called 'hero'."

"Tell me!" said Tom, advancing closer until the tip of his blade touched the pirate's throat.

Sanpao shook his head mockingly, and he spread his arms. His right hand still wore the gauntlet. "Surely you wouldn't hurt an unarmed man?"

Then the Pirate King's gaze flicked slightly to Tom's left. He spun around to find himself face to face with two pirates. One held a boathook, the other a cat-o'nine-tails spiked with pieces of jagged glass.

"Deal with him!" said Sanpao, rushing up the gangplank and onto the deck.

Tom gripped his shield.

The first pirate swung the boathook, and Tom ducked beneath it, lurching forward. He caught the pirate in the belly with the edge of his shield and his enemy dropped to the ground, wheezing. The second lashed with the 'cat', and Tom raised his sword. The nine strands of deadly leather wrapped around his blade. Tom yanked backwards, severing them all.

"Look out!" yelled Elenna.

Tom peered up and saw two more pirates heaving a barrel over the edge of the deck. He jumped sideways as it came crashing down, smashing open on the ground and spilling rum across the clearing. A moment later, and Tom would have been crushed.

"Weigh anchor and away!" bellowed Sanpao.

More pirates were beginning to pull the gangplank back on board, but a stream of arrows from Elenna's bow sent them scurrying for cover. Tom bounded up, leaping onto the deck as the ship began to rise from the ground.

Sanpao was ready for him, cutlass drawn. "Don't you ever give up?" he sighed.

"Not while there's blood in my veins!" said Tom.

Sanpao lunged at him, aiming fierce swipes of his cutlass and driving Tom back against the deck-rail. Tom twisted away from a blow that would have cleaved his head in two, and the cutlass blade sank into the wood. He smacked the flat of his own blade against Sanpao's legs and the pirate buckled. He tried to strike out with the poisoned gauntlet, but Tom met the blow with his shield. The gauntlet

fell loose on the deck between them. Sanpao freed his blade and aimed a cut at Tom's head. He blocked with his own sword and the blades sparked as they clashed. Tom leaned all his strength against Sanpao, pushing him back. Their faces were close.

"You'll never save your king," said the pirate through gritted teeth. "There's no way to stop the poison spreading."

Tom raised a foot and delivered a vicious kick to Sanpao's chest, sending him reeling across the deck. The rising ship was already level with the low branches of the trees. Tom thought fast, stooping to grab the gauntlet carefully. A rope was hanging loose from the rigging. Sanpao grimaced from where he lay on the deck. "Looks like you're coming with us whether you like it or not!" he wheezed.

There'll be time to deal with him later, Tom thought.

He buried his sword in its scabbard and seized the loose rope with his free hand. Then he swung out over the side of the ship, the ground looming below. Tom let go of the rope, turning over in a backwards somersault as he plummeted towards the ground. He landed neatly in the clearing, just as Elenna came rushing over. The pirate ship rose over the trees.

"They're getting away!" she said.

Tom showed her the poisoned gauntlet. "It doesn't matter," he said. "We've got what we need. Let's get back to camp!"

CHAPTER FIVE

A RACE FOR LIFE

Storm's flanks were heaving from the gallop as they arrived back at the tournament ground.

"I'll check on Hugo," said Elenna, and ran off with Silver towards the king's pavilion.

Tom rushed straight to Aduro's tent, gauntlet in hand. He knew that if anyone could identify the poison, it was the former Wizard.

Aduro set to work at once with Daltec, testing the substance on the gauntlet with magic and potions. Neither of them seemed surprised that Sanpao had re-emerged from hiding, and for the moment it didn't matter. Saving King Hugo's life was their priority. It was almost dusk when Elenna came to report that the king was delirious and unable to stand up.

"Captain Harkman says Hugo won't eat or drink," she said. "He raves angrily at anyone who comes near. Not like himself at all."

"How long does he have left?" Tom asked the former Wizard.

Aduro's face was grey with weariness and worry. "A day at best," he answered.

"Got it!" said Daltec, suddenly

standing up. He held aloft a thick leather-bound book he had magically transported all the way from the palace library. "The poison is skolodine!"

Aduro gasped. "Are you sure?"

Tom didn't like the grave look he noticed on Aduro's face. "What is

skolodine?" he asked.

"It a foul slime that can seep through a person's skin," Aduro said, his shoulders stooping. "It can eat away at their goodness, turning them to Evil."

"So how can we prevent that from happening?" asked Tom.

Daltec's eyes scanned the book eagerly. "It says here that skolodine is only found on the walls of the Darkmaw Caves, south of Spindrel. A precious rock is also located there, which, when ground to dust, can be used to make an antidote."

"What does it look like?" asked Elenna.

Daltec frowned. "The book doesn't say, exactly – only that there's a single rock which has been there for hundreds of years."

"We'll set off at once," said Tom, trying to shrug off the cloak of despair that rested heavy on his shoulders.

"Very well," said Aduro. "But be careful. The Darkmaw Caves are…" He paused. "Dangerous. Even the miners won't go in any more."

"Dangerous?" said Elenna. "How?"

Aduro's old eyes glittered in the candlelight. "The caves are fragile. The miners told stories of rockfalls and collapses, and people being trapped without air…"

"And…?" Tom said. "There's something else, isn't there?"

Aduro nodded, and the shadows played over his lined face, making him look older still. "Legend tells of a Beast guardian," he said. "One who guards the caves jealously and without mercy. Of course, it might be just a story."

"It doesn't matter," said Tom, feeling a chill down his spine. "If there's a Beast, we'll deal with it. While there's blood in my veins, we will save King Hugo!"

They left with Storm on foot, so as not to wake the rest of the camp.

The less the courtiers know about this, the better, thought Tom. It was cold, and their breath made clouds in the air. As soon as they were clear of the tents, he and Elenna mounted and set Storm at a gallop along the Southern Road, following a map Daltec had given them. The Darkmaw Caves were a long ride away, around the other side of the Spindrel mountain.

Storm was breathing hard by the time they'd left the city behind, and

rounded the curve of the mountain's
base. On this side, the slopes were
covered in a black swathe of forest
and, even with his magical sight,
Tom's gaze could barely penetrate
the darkness between the trunks.
He noticed that Silver threw the

occasional glance that way, his hackles rising as if he were anxious.

"What do you think will happen if we can't find the antidote?" asked Elenna when they'd ridden a short distance, skirting the forest's edge.

"I don't want to think about that," Tom replied. "A kingdom ruled by an Evil king turns rotten itself. We must succeed. We have to."

A rustling in the branches made them both turn.

"Pirates?" Elenna mouthed.

Tom didn't take his eyes from the trees. He made a signal to his friend with his hands. *Split up. Surround them.*

Elenna nodded and they slipped from Storm's saddle and took a flank each, creeping to the forest's edge.

Tom saw a figure lurking behind a

tree, completely bathed in shadow.
He drew his sword silently. The man
was looking towards where they'd left
Storm and Silver. He wore a crossbow
on his back, and he hadn't seen them
yet.

"Don't move!" shouted Tom. The
figure spun around, and could not see
Elenna leaping from behind him. She
swung her bow into the back of his
legs.

The figure howled in pain and
landed on his backside. As he did,
a shaft of moonlight between the
branches caught his blond hair
and face. It was the boy from the
tournament.

"Shawn!" said Tom.

The boy's face darkened in a blush.

"What are you doing here?" asked
Elenna, shouldering her bow and

offering a hand to help him up. "You
could have got yourself killed!"

Shawn ignored her offer of help
and clambered gingerly to his feet.
"I know something's going on.
You're off on an adventure, aren't

you? Thought you might need some assistance."

"Well, we don't," said Tom sharply. *I can't afford to be worrying about this boy while I'm battling a Beast.*

"King Hugo's sick, isn't he?" said Shawn. "I'm not stupid. I've seen all the worried faces and the scurrying around his tent. If he's ill, people should know."

Tom sheathed his sword and pointed at Shawn's chest. "Now you listen to me," he said. "Whatever you think you know, you're wrong. Don't go spreading rumours."

A slow grin spread over Shawn's face. "Let me come on the adventure, then. I can't spread anything if I'm by your side, can I?"

Tom saw Elenna roll her eyes. "That sounds like blackmail," she muttered.

Shawn shrugged. "Hey, I'm just a concerned subject, like you," he said. "So, what do you say – can I come? You know I'm a brilliant shot. Whatever you're fighting, I'll be useful."

Tom and Elenna shared an anxious look. *We don't have much of a choice*, Tom thought.

"All right," he said. "But stay back if there's any trouble, and always do exactly what Elenna and I say. Got it?"

"Deal!" said Shawn. "Now where are we heading?"

"The Darkmaw Caves," said Tom. "We need something from inside."

Shawn swallowed nervously.

"Still want to come?" said Elenna.

Shawn's smile was so fake it almost made Tom laugh.

"Of course," said Shawn. He turned and marched back towards the road. "Follow me – I know the way!"

Tom shook his head. *He's acting like the leader already! This Quest has just got a lot more complicated…*

CHAPTER SIX

THE MINES OF SPINDREL

Even Storm wasn't big enough to carry the three of them, so Tom decided they would all walk at his side.

Storm might need his strength later, thought Tom.

They plodded on through the night, and through the rising sun of dawn. The mountain was much larger than it looked, and each time they rounded the curve of its base, more road stretched out endlessly in front of them. Silver seemed to have boundless energy, running scouting missions ahead before doubling back. Tom, as always, was glad to have the brave wolf at their side.

The sun had almost reached its peak when they spied a huge black hole gaping in the mountainside, and Tom was dusty and sweaty from the long slog under the sun's fierce glare. The opening looked like a mouth of jagged, broken teeth, at least fifty paces across. Old broken-down carts were scattered about, along with rusted pulley mechanisms and pieces of tattered rope. Tom could just about make out twin metal tracks across the ground, overgrown and buried completely in some places. The mines must once

have been very impressive.

"We're here!" said Shawn. "Told you I knew the way."

He began to stride out ahead, clambering up the slope towards the opening.

Tom checked the map and saw there was a stream a stone's throw further along the path.

"Wait!" he said. "Let's fill up our

water flasks first."

Shawn looked back. "Aren't you supposed to be some sort of hero?" he asked. "Surely you can wait for a drink!"

Tom growled low in his throat. *Why did we let him come?*

"Don't let him get to you," said Elenna. "Come on, let's get a drink."

Tom nodded. As they walked towards the stream together, he muttered, "Shawn's being foolish. He'll need his strength in the mines."

He stooped at the bank, cupping his hands in the water, and gulped down several mouthfuls. Glancing back, he saw Shawn scrambling between the huge boulders at the cave mouth. A sudden movement caught Tom's eye, as three men emerged from behind one of the boulders.

Tom jumped to his feet. Weren't the mines supposed to be deserted?

One of the men clutched a dagger and another held a pickaxe. The third was unarmed. Shawn stumbled backwards, reaching for his crossbow, but the two armed men seized him quickly and spun him round. One placed the dagger at his throat. Even without his magical helmet, Tom could see the fear in Shawn's eyes.

Tom rushed back from the bank, hand on the hilt of his sword. He didn't draw it. What was the point? *Whoever these bandits are, they have the upper hand.*

Elenna followed, her bow and arrow angled at the ground. The men's gaunt faces were set hard. Tom judged them to be about the same age as his uncle Henry – too old to be soldiers,

probably. They looked more desperate
than angry.

Miners, perhaps?

"We mean no harm!" Tom called.
"We just need to go inside the mines."

"No chance!" replied the skinniest of
the men. "These are our caves!"

Shawn wriggled in their grasp, but

they held him firm.

"I thought no one mined here any more," said Elenna.

The men looked at one another shiftily, then the thin one replied, "The pirate said what's inside is ours. As much crystal as we can carry, he promised, as a reward."

Sanpao! Tom was losing patience. They couldn't afford this delay. *We need straight answers.* "Reward for what?" he demanded.

"Never you mind," said the other bandit. "If you know what's good for you, you'll turn back to wherever you came from."

Tom sensed the threats were empty. He whispered to Elenna, "They're afraid. Sanpao must have threatened them."

The unarmed man stooped for a

moment, and dragged a knapsack from behind one of the boulders. He began to tie it hurriedly, but as he did so, Tom caught sight of something inside – something smooth, shiny and lilac.

That doesn't look like crystal to me, he thought, frowning.

"Hey! What is that?" he asked, pointing at the man with the knapsack.

Before the man could answer, the sound of scattering rocks made everyone look to the cave mouth, as a small flurry of pebbles tumbled from the entrance.

Aduro said the mines were fragile, Tom thought.

"See, Arthur?" said the man with the pickaxe to his companion holding Shawn. "I told you I heard something inside. Let's get out of here!"

Arthur lowered his dagger a fraction

from Shawn's neck, then narrowed his eyes at Tom. "No chance," he said. "If we leave, these thieves will take our crystal."

Tom heard a voice in his head. It was full of fury.

I've kept that egg safe for one hundred years…and I want it back!

"Tom, are you all right?" asked Elenna. Tom glanced at the others. No one had heard the voice but him, which meant it was coming through the red jewel in his belt – Torgor's ruby. The words were those of a Beast!

He drew his sword, glancing about, but he could see nothing. *So that's what's in the sack – a Beast's egg!*

"Hey, put down your blade!" said Arthur.

"You need to get away from here," Tom said urgently. "There's something bad inside the caves, and it's coming this way."

The man sneered. "A likely story. The only thing inside is riches. Why don't you— OWWWW!"

He let out a howl as Shawn stamped hard on his foot and slipped from his grasp. But instead of running back towards Tom and Elenna, Shawn headed for the cave entrance.

"Shawn, not that…" Tom began.

His words lodged in his throat as a huge shape emerged from the cave mouth. Shawn's feet skidded out from beneath him and he landed on his back with a cry of terror. Arthur and his companions froze to the spot.

Enormous pincers reached from a segmented body covered in sleek, dark shell. Antennae twitched over the Beast's glittering eyes. Clacking

jaws gaped. It looked like a massive
centipede, one which could flatten
buildings or crush people like ants.

The voice returned to Tom's head,
booming with fury.

You invade the lair of Skolo… You steal
from me… You will pay a terrible price!

CHAPTER SEVEN

THE BEAST WITHIN

"Run!" Elenna shouted.

Shawn scrambled to his feet. Too late. Skolo's claw darted out, closed on his leg and hoisted him upside down in front of her mouthparts.

Tom charged past the stunned men, brandishing his sword. "Let him go!" he cried.

Skolo skittered around on stubby splayed legs, and wings bristled from

her shoulders. As Tom swung his
sword at her shell, the wings fluttered.

Clang!

Jarring pain shot up Tom's arm as
the blade hit metal.

Those wings are made of steel! he
realised with a shock.

Before Tom could attack again, Skolo had darted back inside the cave at incredible speed, dragging Shawn with her. The boy's screams echoed from the darkness.

Tom ran after them, the meagre light catching on the Beast's glinting wings. He saw them scrape across the tunnel walls, and the cave shook as rocks crumbled from above. Dust and debris showered around him, but Tom stumbled on. *I can't let the Beast take Shawn.*

Ahead, Skolo spread her wings, battering the sides of the cave and dislodging huge sections of stone. The rumbling grew louder as the roof above began to break apart.

A hand caught Tom's shoulder and tugged him back.

"Stop!" said Elenna. "You'll get

yourself killed!"

Sure enough, several huge boulders thumped to the ground just ahead – where Tom would have been standing if his friend hadn't grabbed him in time. As the dust cleared, he saw the tunnel was completely blocked.

"Shawn..." he murmured.

The preening boy had been a nuisance, but he didn't deserve a fate like that.

"Come on!" said Elenna. "There must be another way in."

Tom followed her back towards the light. Arthur and his companions were creeping away from the cave mouth, looking sheepish. Elenna whistled and Silver rushed at them, teeth bared and snarling. They pressed their backs together, knees trembling.

"Please, don't let him hurt us!" cried

Arthur desperately.

Tom knew the wolf would never attack without Elenna's word, but Silver certainly looked frightening as he corralled the men.

"Then tell us another route into the caves," said Elenna.

"I… I don't know," said Arthur.

Silver pressed closer with a growl.

"Don't give us that," said Tom. "Sanpao must have looked into every inch of these caves. He wouldn't take a Beast lightly."

Arthur swallowed nervously. "If that pirate knew about the Beast, he never told us!"

Tom was almost certain that the miner wasn't lying. "Tell us more," he said. "What exactly did the pirate say to you?"

Arthur nodded at the wolf. "It's hard

to think with that thing slavering in
front of me."

"Silver, off," said Elenna.

The wolf sat back on his haunches,
suddenly relaxed, with his tongue
lolling.

Arthur breathed a sigh of relief.
"He made us take him into the mines
to look for crystals," he said. "But

when we were down there, he just disappeared along one of the tunnels with an empty bag. Came back with it full. After that he said we could have all the crystals we wanted."

The skolodine was what Sanpao was after, Tom thought. *He took these men down with him for protection, in case they encountered the Beast. Clever, but cruel.*

He walked to Elenna's side and whispered in her ear. "So now we have to rescue Shawn, find the antidote, and work out how to defeat Skolo."

Elenna's mouth was set in a grim line. "While there's blood in our veins, we can do it," she said.

Tom looked over towards the cave mouth. "First of all, we've got to find a way in," he said determinedly.

STORY TWO

The light...take it away! Even the dimmest of candles burns my eyes! The pain gnaws at my insides like an animal eager to get out. Bring me water, someone!

Time means little to me in my agony. The tournament might have been a day ago or a month. In this dark tent it's hard to tell.

My body is wasting. I cannot eat. This poison will be my death.

Only one hope remains. Tom. But this may be a Quest too far, even for him.

Let me sleep. Please, let me sleep.

King Hugo

CHAPTER ONE

DEALING WITH THE BEAST

The sun beat down on all of them – it was almost unbearably hot beneath its glare. Tom pointed to the miner clutching the knapsack. "What is that thing?" he said.

Arthur stepped in front of his companion, sweat trailing from his brow. "None of your business. We've told you everything we know."

"Not yet, you haven't," said Tom. "Perhaps you need Silver to persuade you?"

On cue, the wolf curled his lip menacingly.

"But we found it fair and square," said Arthur, wiping the sweat away with his sleeve. "Selling it might make all this worthwhile. What gives you the right to steal from us? I say we go our separate ways – how about it?"

Elenna leant closer to Tom and whispered, "What do we do?"

Tom narrowed his eyes at the bag. He was sure that he had seen an egg. A Beast's egg. It was too risky to take it by force, because it could so easily break – and how furious would Skolo be then?

"The Beast wants what's in that

bag," he whispered back. "Perhaps if we return it to her, she'll release Shawn." *If he's even still alive*.

Elenna nodded. "Follow my lead," she said.

She walked away from Tom, towards the group of miners. But something was wrong – she was half-stumbling, her head wobbling from side to side.

"Please…" Elenna muttered. "Water…"

When she neared the man with the knapsack, she staggered forward and collapsed to her knees. Silver let out a plaintive howl and rushed to her side.

"Help her!" Tom said, understanding Elenna's plan. "She's got heatstroke. Does anyone have any water?"

The miner with the knapsack looked to the others, then placed his bag on the floor to untie the water-skin at his waist. Elenna managed to stand, using him for support, and as she did so she tucked one foot within the loop of the knapsack's drawstring.

She sipped the water and turned to Tom with a wink.

"Ready?" she said.

Tom nodded. The miners were still frowning in confusion as Elenna flicked her leg and sent the knapsack arcing backwards towards Tom.

"Hey!" shouted Arthur. Tom caught it, cushioning the impact as best he could, then ran back towards Storm.

"Thanks for the water!" said Elenna, rushing to join him.

"Come back here!" cried the miner who'd lost the sack.

Tom spurred Storm into a gallop as soon as Elenna was in the saddle. In no time they'd left the angry miners behind.

"That was good thinking," said Tom, as he slowed Storm to a halt. He opened the knapsack and carefully looked inside. Sure enough, it contained a lilac egg the size of his head.

"No wonder Skolo's furious," he said. "They took one of her young!"

"The sooner we can return it, the sooner we can get on with the proper Quest," said Elenna. "Finding the antidote."

They both dismounted to search for another entrance in the mountainside. There were plenty of small caves, but each proved disappointing, ending after a few paces. Tom was beginning to wonder if they'd ever find a way in.

But at last Silver came darting out of one tunnel with a yelp.

"He's found something!" said Elenna. As they approached the new cave, a narrow tunnel with dripping, jagged rocks on the roof, she frowned. "We've come a long way from the first entrance. How will we even find Skolo and Shawn?"

Tom tapped the ruby in his belt. "I'll use this," he said. "When we get close to them, I'll know."

Storm ducked his head under the tunnel entrance, nostrils flaring. Tom held up a hand. "You stay out here, old friend," he said. "Run at the first sign of trouble."

Storm whinnied. *He doesn't like being left behind*, Tom thought, as he led the way into the mine.

The first thing that hit him was the smell – the same bitter stench as the poison on Sanpao's gauntlets. Looking up to the cave roof, he saw that it was coated in something black and tar-like. "Skolodine," he said, pointing. "Sanpao must have scraped it from the walls of this place."

He pressed on, trying to stay as far from the walls as possible. *I wonder how many miners became poisoned working down here*, he thought.

As they went deeper, tiny sparkling crystals began to appear embedded in the walls, like a night sky filled with stars. Then they passed into further darkness, eyes straining.

The tunnels twisted, rose and fell, and forked into numerous passageways. Tom made sure he memorised their route. It made him shudder to think they could get lost in this dark, poisonous maze.

Soon the utter blackness made it impossible to see at all. Silver led the way, nosing at the air to check for danger. Elenna took the lead with one hand on the wolf's head, and Tom followed with his hand on her shoulder. *Anything could be watching us from the shadows…*

It wasn't long, though, before he saw light ahead, and slowed his steps, drawing his sword a fraction. He made out the tunnel walls once more, slimy and covered in the same black gunge. They rounded a corner and he gasped.

The tunnel opened out into a large cavern, the walls littered with huge chunks of crystal that lit the darkness.

Enough to make a thousand miners

rich, Tom guessed. But it wasn't the crystal that gripped his attention. Pinned to the wall opposite by thick strands of purplish slime, was Shawn.

His eyes locked onto them and he gave an exaggerated sigh.

"About time you two showed up!" he grumbled. "I've been trapped down here for ages!"

Tom raised a finger to his lips to

shush him, but Shawn didn't seem to notice. "Come on, Tom. Put that sword of yours to some use and get me…"

A rattling sound silenced him at last. It came from another tunnel leading from the cavern.

Skolo had heard them.

She was coming.

CHAPTER TWO

CAVE FIGHT

The giant winged centipede burst
from the tunnel with a shriek. Her
mouthparts gaped and more purple
strands shot from her throat. Tom
held up his shield and felt the slime
smack into its surface and rip it from
his arm. The shield landed on the
ground with a splat. He tried to pick
it up, but it wouldn't budge. Skolo
fired again, coating his boot. Pain

shot through Tom's knee as he tried
to move. It was no good: his foot was
stuck to the ground!

The Beast surged towards him, and he felt the jaw pincers close around his middle. He was lifted into the air, leaving one boot still stuck to the ground.

Where is my egg? Skolo's voice screamed in Tom's head. *You and your companions stole it from me!*

"Give her the egg!" Tom cried.

As Skolo shook him back and forth, he saw Elenna draw the lilac egg from the knapsack and hold it aloft. "Here!" she shouted. "It's here!"

Skolo hurled Tom so he crashed into the cave wall, the air exploding from his lungs. Lying, breathless, on his side, Tom saw the Beast stalk towards Elenna.

Thief! she cried. *All humans are thieves!*

"She doesn't understand!" Tom

called to his friend. "Keep your distance."

"What about me?" shouted Shawn. "Don't forget about me!"

Elenna backed away from Skolo, still holding the egg at arm's length. The Beast's wings trembled with fury, and her pincers snapped in front of her. Elenna seemed to realise the

danger she was in, and backed off into another tunnel, too narrow for Skolo to follow. The Beast surged after her, but her body ground to a halt, lodged halfway into the passage

Tom managed to stand, and quickly rushed to retrieve his boot. The Beast squirmed to get free, wings straining and legs scraping the ground.

Tom had just recovered his shield when, with a grinding sound, Skolo's metal wings cut through the rock and she backed up into the cavern. The tunnel ceiling fell in a shower of rock, trapping Elenna on the other side.

Skolo shook the dust free from her shell and swivelled to face Tom. With her egg lost on the other side of the collapse, she looked angrier than ever.

"We're your friends," Tom said, both aloud and through the red jewel. "We're not here to hurt you."

"Ha!" said Shawn. "Good luck with that approach."

Skolo cocked her head, eyes full of intelligence, and for a moment Tom dared to hope that she'd understood. But then she scuttled quickly to the large tunnel through which she'd approached. With her blade-like wings a blur, she hacked at the rock as she charged through. The tunnel crumbled and collapsed behind her, blocking their only escape route.

The Beast's hissing voice burrowed into Tom's head.

You will die in here!

"Will you please help me out of

this?" said Shawn.

Tom ignored him, and ran quickly to the fallen tunnel which Elenna had gone down. Now the dust had cleared, he could see a few tiny gaps between the rocks.

"Hey!" said Shawn. "Are you even listening?"

Tom scrambled over the debris and put his mouth to one of the cracks. "Elenna?" he said.

"I'm all right," she replied. Her face appeared beyond. "Where's Skolo?"

"She's trapped us in here," he said. "I don't know where she's gone. But we can be sure she knows this network of caves better than anyone."

"I'll try to find her," said Elenna. "Maybe she'll accept the egg this time."

"I'm not sure that's a good idea,"

said Tom. "It's too dangerous."

Elenna sighed. "There's no other choice, is there?"

Shawn chuckled. "Are you two always this pathetic?" he asked. "Aren't you supposed to have killed lots of Beasts?"

"Defeated, not killed," said Tom. "And have you forgotten that it was you who got us into this mess? If you hadn't rushed off—"

"Tom!" hissed Elenna. "Listen…"

He heard it too. The scuttle of the Beast's feet. But where was it coming from?

With a stab of terror, he realised. "Elenna, she's coming for you," he said.

Elenna spun around, and beyond his friend Tom could see Skolo's shadow creeping towards her.

"Give her the egg!" he said.

As Elenna extended her trembling arms towards Skolo, Tom pressed the red jewel.

Don't hurt her, he said to the Beast. *She has what you want.*

He heard the clacking mouthparts, and the low hum of the Beast's scything wings. Then Elenna let out a piercing scream. It cut off with a *splat!*

"Elenna?" Tom said.

There was no reply.

CHAPTER THREE

SEARCHING FOR ELENNA

Silver let out a sad whine and pawed at the rocks.

"Is she all right?" asked Shawn, sounding suddenly serious.

Tom pulled Silver away. "Down, boy," he soothed. "Let me."

He harnessed the power of the golden gauntlets and punched at the rockfall. Pain lanced through his

hand, but he gritted his teeth and punched again, smashing the rock. Desperation drove him on. *I've got to get to my friend.*

Clawing and punching, he tore at the collapsed stone, eventually making a hole large enough to crawl through. His hands were bleeding. Silver scampered through and howled. Tom went after him, and his heart lurched. Elenna, and the egg, were gone, and the rocks were coated with the purple slime.

He crouched beside Silver, who was desperately sniffing the ground.

"Skolo's taken her," he muttered. "But we'll get her back, I promise."

"Helloooo?" called Shawn. "Anybody?"

Tom fought to suppress his anger. *I can't just leave him, even though it would make this whole Quest much simpler.*

He climbed back through the opening and rushed to Shawn's side, drawing his sword as he approached. His face must have looked furious, because Shawn starting jabbering, "Hey, take it easy, huh? We'll get your friend back..."

Lifting his blade above his head,

Tom brought it down hard on the strands of purple Beast-slime. Shawn fell free.

"Thanks! Phew! For a moment there I thought you were going to…"

"I thought about it," said Tom. "Now listen to me – from now on, you follow my orders. The first one is, don't run off. Got it?"

"Now, hang on," said Shawn, following Tom through the gap and into the tunnel. "Who made you the…"

Silver jumped up, planting his paws on Shawn's chest and pinning him against the wall. He leant close to Shawn's face.

The boy grinned uneasily. "All right. I've got it, boss."

Silver let him go, and together they set off down the tunnel where Skolo had taken Elenna. The walls were scarred with deep gouges from the Beast's wings, and coated with more black gunge. Silver paced ahead, ears pricked for any sound.

Tom listened intently through Torgor's red jewel, but heard nothing. *Either the Beast isn't nearby, or she's laying a trap in silence.*

"You know, I could probably have taken the Beast on myself," said Shawn. "I'd just worked out an escape plan."

"Really?" said Tom, eyes scanning the darkness ahead. "You looked fairly tied up to me."

"I was just tricking the Beast into thinking the same," said Shawn. "But actually—"

Silver growled, nosing the air, and Tom held up a hand to silence Shawn.

The tunnel curved ahead and Tom drew his sword.

"Stay back," he whispered.

Shawn nodded, but Silver sat in front of him anyway, just in case.

Tom crept forward, shield lowered onto his arm. As he rounded the corner, the first thing he saw was Elenna lying on the ground,

unconscious and bleeding from a cut on her head. "She's in here!" he said.

Silver and Shawn joined him as he rushed to kneel at her side. He put his hand under her nose, and relief flooded his chest. She was breathing. Silver nuzzled at her neck and her eyelids flickered.

"Uh-oh," said Shawn.

Tom followed the boy's gaze. Lying
on the floor a few paces away were
several fragments of lilac eggshell.
Skolo's young had hatched!

CHAPTER FOUR

DEADLY OFFSPRING

Elenna's arms bore scratches and cuts. "She must have been fighting the Beast bravely," Tom said.

"Or perhaps her offspring," said Shawn. He was playing with the eggshell, turning it over in his hands.

"Stop messing around and help me," said Tom.

Shawn tossed the shell aside, and together they took hold of Elenna

139

under the armpits and dragged her toward the tunnel wall where she could sit upright. The gash on her head was deep and her skin was pale from blood loss. Tom didn't think she'd been bitten, though.

As they leaned her against the wall, her hands shot out, raking at Tom's face. "Get off me!" she cried, as if she were still battling against the Beast.

Tom fought to control her as she punched and kicked. Then her eyes flew open.

"What? Tom..."

"It's all right," he said. "Lie still. Skolo has gone."

Elenna glanced around, eyes full of relief. "Gone?" she muttered. Tom nodded and Elenna continued. "It hatched," she said. "And straight away it began to grow. It was twice the size in no time at all. I tried to calm it but it was scurrying about madly. It's quick, and powerful. I couldn't..." Her eyes rolled back in her head, and she almost lost consciousness again.

"Don't try to speak," said Tom, supporting her head as he leaned her against the wall by the broken pieces of eggshell. "You've taken a few knocks. I'll use the phoenix talon."

Leaving Silver and Shawn to guard her, Tom detached Epos's magical healing talon from his shield.

I hope it's just cuts and bruises, Tom thought. *If there's any skolodine in her bloodstream, the talon will be next to useless*. But before he could even hold it against Elenna's head, the gash seemed to be closing of its own accord, right before his eyes. Miraculously, the cuts on her arms had vanished already. The flush of health returned to her skin.

"What's happening?" asked Shawn. "That's impossible!"

Tom's eyes landed on the shattered egg and the truth hit him like a thunderbolt. "It's magic," he said. "Now I understand. The eggshell is the precious rock Daltec mentioned!

It can heal the king too!"

"Of course!" said Elenna, standing and stretching her limbs. "Daltec said it hadn't been seen for hundreds of years. Skolo must have been guarding her egg all that time."

"No wonder she was angry when those miners stole it," said Shawn.

Tom picked up a piece of the shell. It was almost warm to the touch and perfectly smooth. He tucked it inside his tunic. "You should each take a piece too," he said. "That way we have triple the chance of getting some safely back to the king."

Elenna and Shawn did so, and with Silver leading the way, they headed along the tunnel.

"Are you sure this is the way out?" asked Shawn after a short time.

No, thought Tom, *but what other*

option do we have?

They reached a fork he thought he recognised. One branch definitely looked familiar.

"Follow me," he said.

After a few hundred paces, Tom grinned. They'd reached the section with the sparkling crystals in the walls, which meant they were almost back in the open air. He did a quick mental calculation. *We should be back at the royal camp by noon.*

Silver stopped in his tracks, whining nervously.

"Oh no…" said Elenna.

A smaller version of Skolo blocked the passage ahead. The creature was almost identical, but for a slightly narrower body. Though by no means as large as Skolo herself, he was still the size of a market cart, with jaws

big and powerful enough to take off
an arm or leg with ease.

He trembled, then gave a hissing
squeal. As they watched, his skin
stretched and his body swelled again,
increasing in size.

"He's still growing!" said Elenna.

The Beast reared, rising on his hind
legs and snapping his mandibles
together. Two stubby wings, so thin

they were almost translucent, burst
from his back. Tom sensed a wave
of emotions through the ruby. *Fear.
Confusion. Panic.*

"He's still too young to understand
what's happening," he told the others.

"Of course!" said Elenna. "He
probably wasn't meant to be born
today. All the jostling must have
made him hatch early!"

Shawn unhooked his crossbow and
pointed it at the young Beast. "He'll
understand this!"

"No!" said Tom and Elenna
together.

Tom pushed the bow down. "Idiot!"
he said. "You'll bring the mother!"

"Too late," said Elenna, pointing
behind him.

Tom spun around and saw the huge
form of the Beast barrelling down the

tunnel towards them.

Don't hurt my baby! her voice
screamed in Tom's head.

The Beast had come to rescue her
young.

And they were right in her path.

147

CHAPTER FIVE

ENTANGLED

Skolo skidded to a halt a few paces away, and her mouthparts twitched.

"She's going to fire her slime!" Elenna cried. "Duck!"

Tom shoved Shawn against the tunnel wall and flattened himself to the ground as the streaks of purple ooze shot over his head.

He heard a muffled sound and turned to see Skolo's offspring struggling with the slime on one of his pincers, glued to the wall.

Skolo has hit her own child!

Tom gripped the red jewel and willed his words into Skolo's head. *Stop this!* he said to her. *We're not your enemies. Let me help.*

Taking a risk, he climbed to his feet, staring all the time at Skolo. He backed slowly towards her offspring, shield at the ready, but sword sheathed. He didn't want to appear a threat. Skolo watched him, eyes blazing. If Tom could free her young, perhaps she would trust him.

Psst!

An arrow sang through the air from Shawn's crossbow and thudded into the Beast's shell. Skolo roared in pain and bucked against the tunnel wall, snapping the shaft off in her flesh.

Shawn began to reload from his quiver.

"Stop firing, you idiot!" yelled Elenna.

Skolo fluttered her wings, making the whole tunnel shake. More slime darted from her jaws, spraying everywhere. Tom dodged and raised

151

his shield, deflecting a strand that would have struck Shawn. Elenna weaved from side to side, and Silver whined as a globule caught his paws, sticking them together and leaving him flailing on his back

"What do we do?" asked Elenna, rushing to Silver's side.

"We use her own weapons against

her," said Tom, drawing his sword. Harnessing the power of the golden boots, he hurled himself towards the Beast at super-speed. Strands of slime shot past his head, but he managed to catch one on his sword hilt. He dropped into a slide, sailing right between Skolo's front legs on his back, dragging the gooey slime

with him. He wrapped it around her back legs then darted back again to entangle her front legs too, stretching the strands as he went. Skolo bellowed and twitched as she tried to follow his movements, but Tom was already on the move, running up the tunnel wall. He somersaulted backwards, dragging the strands over her wings as he went. By the time he landed, they were glued to her back. The Beast was well and truly trussed up, unable either to move or use her wings.

"All right – that *was* impressive," said Shawn. He picked up his crossbow. "Let's take care of this Evil creature once and for all."

Elenna was on him in a flash, and bent his arm up behind his back. "You've done quite enough," she said.

Skolo was writhing on the ground, mandibles snapping, but Tom stood right in front of her.

It's over, he said to Skolo in his mind, trusting that the ruby would transmit his thoughts. *We aren't here to fight you or do you harm. We aren't the ones who disturbed your sleep or threatened your young. He* – Tom pointed to Shawn – *is a stupid human*

155

and doesn't know what he is doing.

Shawn squirmed in Elenna's grip. "Ouch!" he said. "That hurts!"

The Beast narrowed her eyes.

She's trying to understand, Tom realised.

Let me help your little one, he said. *I'm Avantia's Master of the Beasts.*

For the first time, Skolo's voice was not furious. *The Master?* she asked.

Tom nodded. Hidden away in these caves, he guessed, she might not have seen a Master of the Beasts for hundreds of years. Maybe not since Tanner, the first Master.

Sword drawn, he backed away slowly towards her offspring, still struggling to free his pincer from the tunnel wall.

Trust me… Tom said to both Beasts as, with a sawing motion, he cut the strands that bound the young one. He squirmed free, wings bristling. Tom forced himself to stand firm, even though Skolo's son could kill him in an instant if he wanted to.

"Tom, what are you doing?" asked Elenna, her face alive with panic.

"Earning Skolo's trust," he replied.

The young Beast twitched his jaws, which dripped with purple ooze. Tom held his breath.

But Skolo's offspring didn't attack. Instead he gently brushed Tom's shoulder with a pincer.

He is Good, Mother, the young Beast said. *He is our friend.*

Tom breathed a slow sigh of relief. The young Beast scuttled past him, then past a terrified Shawn, and began to pick at the strands entangling Skolo. Tom joined it,

cutting carefully with his sword.
Soon she too was free, and stood
up, thrashing and tearing at the last
shreds. She turned to face Tom and
his companions, her son sheltering
beneath her legs. Her eyes gleamed as

she reared up, head brushing the top of the cave and wings bristling. Skolo opened her mouth, and her roar shook the ground beneath Tom's feet.

"I thought you said you'd earn her trust!" cried Shawn. "You've failed! We're about to die in here!"

Backing away as he stared up at the looming Beast, Tom wondered if he had made a terrible mistake.

CHAPTER SIX

MASTER OF THE BEASTS

Tom felt sure he would be crushed. Skolo's huge, shelled body would have weighed ten of Storm at least.

But the Beast settled down again just in front of him, lowering her head to his. Her eyes softened a little and her jaws closed in a series of clacks.

Greetings, Master, she said. *You are welcome here in my home.*

Tom's fear evaporated in an instant. He reached out and laid a hand on the hard shell of her head.

"Is it safe?" muttered Shawn.

Tom grinned. "It is now."

Shawn didn't move any closer, but Elenna joined Tom, stroking the pincer of the smaller Beast. Even Silver came near enough for a sniff.

Tom would have liked to spend more time with Skolo and her offspring, but more pressing concerns weighed heavy on his mind. Elenna voiced the same fears.

"We need to get back to King Hugo – immediately!" she said.

Tom backed away from the Beast, clutching the red jewel. *Perhaps we'll meet again*, he said.

You cannot leave, Skolo replied. *It is the duty of the Master to name new Beasts.*

Tom smiled warmly. *I will return with a name, I promise*, he said. *But my first loyalty is to the kingdom and the king.*

With the remaining fragments of eggshell safely stored in the knapsack, Tom asked the Beast, *Can you show us the way out?*

Skolo didn't speak, but she scuttled away down the tunnel, followed by her son. Tom and his companions followed, and soon he saw daylight just ahead.

At the entrance to the mines, Storm waited. He backed off at the sight of the two giant creatures walking ahead of Tom, Elenna and Shawn.

"It's all right, boy," said Tom. "They're Good Beasts."

He climbed onto the stallion's back, and Elenna mounted behind him. By the time he looked back to the cave entrance, the Beasts had gone.

"Hold up!" said Shawn. "What about me?"

Tom looked down sternly at their fellow adventurer. "You've been nothing but trouble from the start," he said. "You can walk back to camp – it should only take a day or so."

"That's not—"

Tom kicked Storm's flanks and the thunder of hooves smothered the rest of Shawn's complaints. Soon they were galloping along the track back towards the camp at Spindrel.

I hope we're not too late, thought Tom, leaning low to the stallion's neck and pushing him hard.

"Tom, look out!" Elenna cried. Her hands snaked over his and jerked the reins sideways. As Storm veered and almost fell, a metal hook swept a

hair's breadth from Tom's face.

"Greetings, me hearties!" bellowed a familiar voice.

Tom looked up and saw Sanpao's ship floating over their heads. It must have approached in silence. Dangling from the deckrails were several vicious boat-hooks, tied to ropes.

Pirates leaned over the side of the vessel. Tom nudged Storm forward to avoid another hook.

"Tear their heads off!" Sanpao cried.

The pirates laughed as several more hooks sliced the air.

"We don't have time for this," Tom growled. "Elenna, take Storm."

"What are *you* going to do?" asked Elenna.

"This!" Tom said.

As a hook swung past, Tom timed its speed perfectly, grabbing the end and letting it lift him from the saddle. Quick as he could, he scrambled up the rope, hand over hand. By the time the Sanpao realised what had happened, Tom was heaving himself onto the deck. He shoved two pirates out of the way with his shield and charged towards the wheel. The

helmsman managed to draw his
cutlass, but Tom swatted it from his
hand with a swipe of his sword. The
defenceless pirate cowered.

"Please, don't kill me!" he cried.

"I'm not going to kill you," said Tom. He turned to see several other crew members running across the deck towards him, including an angry Sanpao.

There's not much time.

He hacked at the wheel with his sword, destroying it in a few cuts. All the pirates, and Tom, skittered across the timbers as the ship leaned dangerously and began to dive towards the ground. Tom scrambled over the rail as the trees of the forest approached at speed.

"Crash-landing!" bellowed Sanpao. "Take cover!"

Tom hesitated long enough to see the terror in the eyes of the Pirate King, then jumped from the plummeting ship into a treetop. Twigs and leaves scratched his arms and

face, but he managed to hold on. The
vessel crashed into the forest with
the sound of breaking branches and
pirates' screams. Sails collapsed and
rigging snapped as the ship came to
rest, prow down, among the trees.

*That should keep them busy with repairs
for a while*, Tom thought. *Now, back to
the king!*

CHAPTER SEVEN

THE EDGE OF DEATH

It didn't take long for Tom to climb down from the tree and find Storm and Elenna. Back in the saddle, he guided the stallion to the path and they set off towards Spindrel.

By the time they galloped back into camp, the mood was sombre. All signs of the tournament had been cleared away, and people stood in small groups, muttering to one another. News of the king's illness had obviously been spreading, despite efforts to keep it secret. Captain Harkman and his knights stood guard outside the royal tent.

"How's the king?" asked Tom, as he dismounted.

The captain had dark shadows beneath his eyes, as though he hadn't slept a wink. "It's bad," he whispered. "Very bad."

Leaving Storm and Silver outside, Tom and Elenna burst into the tent.

Daltec was standing over the king, and Aduro dozed in a chair. Both looked up as Tom entered, taking the eggshell fragment from inside his tunic.

"Tom!" cried Aduro.

"Here's the antidote!" Tom said.

"Are we in time?"

Daltec put the pieces of shell into a
large mortar. "I hope so," he said. He
began to grind the shell at once with
a pestle.

Tom frowned. "Elenna's wounds
were healed just by the touch of the
shell," he said.

"But His Majesty has been ill for too

long," Daltec replied. "The skolodine is working its way through his bloodstream – which means, so must our remedy."

Tom approached the king's bedside slowly and stifled a gasp. He felt Elenna's fingers grip his arm like a claw.

King Hugo seemed to have shrunk inside his clothes, so they hung off

his skeletal frame. His face looked twenty...no, thirty years older – wrinkled and sagging. His hair had turned grey, and his once rich beard was just a few sparse wisps of white.

"The skolodine has ravaged him," said Aduro. He laid his own old hand over the king's bony fingers. "It won't be long before Evil takes over his thoughts and he is lost to us forever."

They waited as Daltec worked, mixing the powdered eggshell with boiling water and other ingredients. Tom crouched beside the king, searching for a pulse beneath the paper-thin skin of his wrist. He wasn't sure he could feel one at all.

"It's ready!" called Daltec. "Move aside."

Tom and Elenna shifted as Daltec rushed over with a small dish. Inside was a creamy pink substance.

"Apply it to his right palm," said Aduro. "That's where the infection started."

Daltec scooped the cream onto the king's hand and straight away it sank into his skin.

"More!" said Aduro.

Daltec obeyed, and soon all the cream was gone.

"Will it be enough?" Elenna asked.

Aduro's face was grave. "Only time will tell. The infection took hold very strongly."

Tom stared intently at King Hugo, willing his withered lips to move. But the first thing he noticed was a smattering of dark hairs appearing across the king's jawline. Next, a pink flush returned to his cheeks.

"It's working!" Daltec cried.

Suddenly the changes came in a rush, as the sunken cheeks filled out and the wrinkles vanished from the king's face, and his body seemed to grow into his clothes once more. His hair darkened and his beard returned. Then his lips parted and the sudden rush of a breath made his chest swell. His eyes blinked open and he frowned at the faces around him.

"What...what happened?" he croaked.

Tom smiled. "It's a long story, Your Majesty."

The camp rejoiced when the king appeared at the entrance to his tent. He was still weak, though, and Aduro advised him to rest for the remainder of the day. By nightfall, King Hugo's appetite had returned, and he sat with Tom, Elenna, Aduro and Daltec around a small table in his tent. They ate a simple meal of fruits and cold meats off a large platter as Tom finished the tale of their latest Quest.

"So, do you think we've seen the last of Sanpao?" asked the king. "Should I send soldiers to search for him and his crew?"

"I think all you will find is the wreck of his ship," said Tom. "The Pirate King has evaded capture so many times, he knows his luck will run out. He'll be long gone by now."

"And this Skolo," asked the king, "why is it we had never heard of her before?"

Daltec shook his head, a blush rising to his cheeks. "It is my fault, Your Majesty," he said with downcast eyes. "I must visit the library more often once we've returned to the capital."

"Without each of you, I would be dead," said the king. "I won't demote you to apprentice just yet," he added, with a wink and a teasing smile.

Tom laid a hand on Daltec's shoulder. "Don't blame yourself," he said. "If there's one thing all my Quests have taught me, it's that there are always new things to learn."

Aduro nodded. "Your father, Taladon, once said something similar. He believed that new experiences were unavoidable and one should not be ashamed of not knowing something. It's how one deals with new challenges that's important."

A wave of sadness swept through Tom. He didn't often dwell on his father's death, but every so often he realised how much he missed him. "May I be excused, Your Majesty?" he asked.

"Of course," said King Hugo, with a solemn nod.

Stepping outside the tent into the cool night, Tom saw that most of the camp had retired to their own beds. He gazed south, in the direction of the Darkmaw Caves. He imagined

Skolo and her offspring together in the tunnels, and remembered the Beast's final words to him, about his duties as Master.

The noise of soft footsteps made him turn. It was Elenna.

"Are you all right?" she asked softly.

"Yes," he said. "Just speaking of Taladon – it made me realise how much he taught me in the short time I knew him."

Elenna grinned and punched his arm lightly. "And he taught you well," she said.

"Thank you," said Tom. "But listen, how would you like to take a ride with me tomorrow, back to the Darkmaw Caves? We can catch up with the royal retinue later."

Elenna nodded. "Why?" she said.

Tom looked at her. An idea had

come to him, as they sat at the table discussing his father. "I promised Skolo I would name her offspring, remember?" he said.

"And you've thought of a name?" asked Elenna.

"I have," Tom replied. "I will call him Talador, after my father."

He kept his eye on the Darkmaw

Caves, the site of his latest Quest – but not his last. He was not nervous about this, though – thanks to him and Elenna, Avantia had a brand new Beast protector.

In his heart, Tom knew that Talador would live up to his name.

Have you read all the books in the
latest Beast Quest series,
THE CURSED DRAGON?
Out now!

FREE COLLECTOR CARDS INSIDE!

Series 14: THE CURSED DRAGON
COLLECT THEM ALL!

Tom must face four terrifying Beasts as he searches for the ingredients for a potion to rescue the Cursed Dragon.

978 1 40832 920 7

978 1 40832 921 4

978 1 40832 922 1

978 1 40832 923 8

Win an exclusive
Beast Quest T-shirt and goody bag!

In every Beast Quest book the Beast Quest logo is
hidden in one of the pictures. Find the logo in this book
and make a note of which page it appears on.
Write the page number on a postcard and
send it in to us.
Each month we will draw one winner to receive
a Beast Quest T-shirt and goody bag.

THE BEAST QUEST COMPETITION:
SKOLO THE BLADED MONSTER
Orchard Books
338 Euston Road, London NW1 3BH
Australian readers should email:
childrens.books@hachette.com.au

New Zealand readers should write to:
Beast Quest Competition
PO Box 3255, Shortland St, Auckland 1140, NZ.
or email: childrensbooks@hachette.co.nz

Only one entry per child.
Closing date: 31 December 2014

You can also enter this competition
via the Beast Quest website: www.beastquest.co.uk

Fight the Beasts,
Fear the Magic

Do you want to know more
about BEAST QUEST?
Then join our Quest Club!

Visit
www.beastquest.co.uk/club
and sign up today!

Series 1

COLLECT THEM ALL!

Have you read all the books in Series 1 of
BEAST QUEST? Read on to find out where
it all began in this sneak peek from book 1,
FERNO THE FIRE DRAGON...

978 1 84616 483 5

978 1 84616 482 8

978 1 84616 484 2

978 1 84616 486 6

978 1 84616 485 9

978 1 84616 487 3

CHAPTER ONE

THE MYSTERIOUS FIRE

Tom stared hard at his enemy. "Surrender, villain!" he cried. "Surrender, or taste my blade!"

He gave the sack of hay a firm blow with the poker. "That's you taken care of," he announced. "One day I'll be the finest swordsman in all of Avantia. Even better than my father, Taladon the Swift!"

Tom felt the ache in his heart that always came when he thought about his father. The uncle and aunt who had brought Tom up since he was a baby never spoke about him or why he had left Tom to their care after Tom's mother had died.

He shoved the poker back into its pack. "One day I'll know the truth," he swore.

As Tom walked back to the village, a sharp smell caught at the back of his throat.

"Smoke!" he thought.

He stopped and looked around. Through the trees to his left, he could hear a faint crackling as a wave of warm air hit him.

Fire!

Tom pushed his way through the trees and burst into a field. The golden wheat had been burned to black stubble and a veil of smoke hung in the air. Tom stared in horror. How had this happened?

He looked up and blinked. For a second he thought he saw a dark shape moving towards the hills in the distance. But then the sky was empty again.

An angry voice called out. "Who's there?"

Through the smoke, Tom saw a figure stamping around the edge of the field.

"Did you come through the woods?" the man demanded. "Did you see who did this?"

Tom shook his head. "I didn't see a soul!"

"There's evil at work here," said the farmer, his eyes flashing. "Go and tell your uncle what's happened. Our village of Errinel is cursed – and maybe all of us with it!"

Read FERNO THE FIRE DRAGON to find out what happens next...